Carlos López Arancet

To my beloved kids

Amelia, Beltrán, Clara and Batista

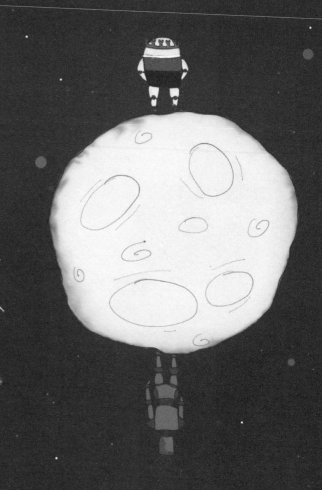

At the far end of the galaxy spun a small blue planet inhabited by two robots: King and Subject.

The planet was so small that if one robot wanted to move about, the other must, too, for there was not enough room for one to stand still.

King, being always quite rude,
often ordered Subject around.

"Subject," he shouted, "move faster! I want to stand
on the other side of the planet!"

King never said, "Please." He never asked Subject
whether he wanted to move, and never thanked him
when he obediently changed places.

One day, King woke up and said, "Subject, I am bored with this small planet. There is not enough room here for an important robot like me. Go out and find a bigger planet for us."

Subject had never left their small planet, and the thought of venturing out into space scared him. What if he got lost, all alone in the galaxy?

But when he asked King whether finding a new planet was truly necessary, King merely replied, "Do not be silly, Subject. Now, do as I say and get me the perfect planet immediately."

Days passed, and King began to grow quite upset.
The planet was even more boring with no one to
give orders to, and he wondered when Subject
would return.

Suddenly, King spied a bright light heading his way.
It was Subject!

Without so much as a greeting, King barked,
"Have you found a new planet?"

"Yes, and it's so big that to get to the other
side you must walk at least fifty steps,"
Subject declared.

"At least fifty steps? That is perfect!
A planet that I truly deserve, not like this small
blue planet! What are you waiting for?
Take me there immediately!" ordered King.

Subject paused. "There is something else I should tell you. The new planet is closer to the sun than our planet, and it is 100 degrees hotter than here."

"100 degrees hotter?" exclaimed King, very upset. "Do you want my circuits to melt? No, that will never do. Go out right now and find me another planet."

Subject's journey had been long, and he was in need of a rest. But he did as he was told. Firing his booster, he sped off to find another planet.

"Don't keep me waiting!" King shouted again.

Several days passed before Subject finally returned. King was by now very upset and bored. His planet was no fun without someone to give orders to. But in truth, he was also quite lonely!

Seeing Subject, King asked, "Have you found another planet?"

"Yes, and it's so big that you will have to shout twice so that I can hear you from the other hemisphere," responded Subject.

"That is not a big problem for me. I like to shout at you," said King, laughing. "So, what are you waiting for? Take me there!"

"There is something else I should tell you," said Subject. "This new planet is much farther from the sun than our planet. It is 100 degrees colder than here."

"100 degrees colder?" shouted King. "Do you want my circuits to freeze? No good. No good at all. Go back right now and find me another planet! This is your last chance Subject. If you cannot find a suitable planet, do not come back!"

Subject, extremely tired, fuelled his thrusters and hurried to complete his mission. "Don't take too long!" King shouted at him again.

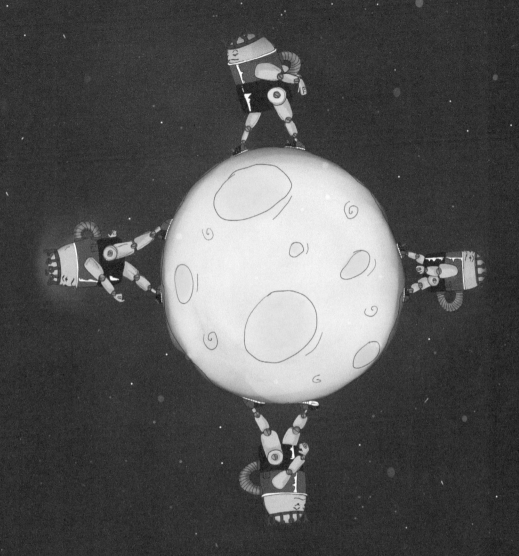

Many days passed, and then many more. Just when King was beginning to wonder whether perhaps Subject wasn't going to come back, he saw a light in the sky.

"Finally!" King exclaimed, somewhat relieved. "Have you found the right place? Not too hot, not too cold?"

"Yes, King. I have found a perfect planet. It's not only bigger, but it's very beautiful—full of flowers, rivers and animals and with the most pleasant temperature you can imagine," Subject replied.

"I knew that I would find the perfect planet!" exclaimed King, "Subject, take me there immediately!"

But Subject shook his head. "Why should I take you there? You are rude. You never say please or thank you. No, I came only to tell you that I will be leaving you behind. You wished for a bigger planet with enough space. Now that I am leaving, this planet will be a better place for you."

And with that, Subject zooted off toward the new planet he had discovered.

Months passed, and King—all alone on the small blue planet—thought about Subject's words. In truth, he regretted the way he had treated his friend. He wondered whether he would ever see him again.

Then one day, King saw
a light in the sky. It was
Subject.

"Oh, Subject!" he shouted
before Subject could say
a word.

"Hello, King. I decided to visit you because I wanted to know how you were after all this time," said Subject.

"I am so sorry, Subject," King replied sadly. "I was never kind or grateful to you. I did not value your company and loyalty. The way I treated you was wrong. I know that now."

"Thank you for visiting me today," King continued. "I never thought that I would have the opportunity to tell you what I have learned—that you are not just Subject. You are my true friend—a friend who deserves to live on the perfect planet."

And Subject, hearing King's words, knew that his robot spirit had genuinely changed forever.

"King, my friend," Subject said, "say no more. It is time to pack your bags. We shall live happily on our perfect planet—together forevermore."

Lightning Source UK Ltd.
Milton Keynes UK
UKHW050830310322
400862UK00002B/50